For Kerry and Leon Cole
W.M.

For Terri
M.B.

Text copyright © 1987 by William Mayne
Illustrations copyright © 1987 by Martin Baynton

Published by Prentice Hall Books for Young Readers, A Division of
Simon & Schuster, Inc.
1230 Avenue of the Americas, New York, NY 10020

10 9 8 7 6 5 4 3 2 1

Prentice Hall Books for Young Readers is a trademark of Simon & Schuster, Inc.

Originally published in Great Britain by Walker Books Ltd, 1987
Printed by L.E.G.O., Vicenza, Italy

Library of Congress Cataloging in Publication Data
Mayne, William, 1928-
Mousewing.
Summary: A mouse with a longing to fly, on seeing two young brothers in danger from an owl,
"flies" down from a roof to save them.
[1. Mice — Fiction]   I. Baynton, Martin, ill.   II. Title.
PZ7.M4736Mp   1988   [E]   87-12437
ISBN 0-13-604240-6

Mousewing

Written by
William Mayne

Illustrated by
Martin Baynton

Prentice Hall Books for Young Readers
A Division of Simon & Schuster, Inc.
New York

Evening, and mice wake up.
Youngmouse sits and watches light grow
dark enough. His eyes are brown; they
watch below.

"What are you thinking?" asks
Mothermouse, "so still and quiet."

"With my eyes I see the garden fall
asleep," says Youngmouse. "Petals fold,
seeds fall. Cat's behind the window."

"Best place for him," says Mothermouse.
"Fathermouse, wake Littlemouse and
Tinymouse. It's time to go looking and
leasing, seeking and gleaning."

They live by the cellar door. People live above, and Cat with starlit eyes.

Youngmouse's eyes are round. They watch above.

"Who is it flying by?" he asks. "It is not Owl. Owl has moonlit eyes."

"That's Flittermouse," his mother says. "Flittermouse may fly."

"I wish I did," says Youngmouse. "I'd not go far or high. Is there a way, Papa?"

"Don't talk of that," his father sharply says. "We don't approve of Flittermouse. He's nothing to admire."

Youngmouse watches Flittermouse. Flittermouse's eyes are night. I wish I could, I wish I did, dreams Youngmouse. Not long, and very low, he sighs.

"Don't think of it," says Fathermouse.

Across the city distantly
calls Owl. Padding down
the street is Cat. Desperate
and serious in drains
the rats are marching.
In the garden all is quiet.
A drip of dew, a drop of nectar, fall from
leaf and flower. Stars hang in the trees.

Fathermouse goes in and out, hearing, peering, sensing with whiskers, feeling with feet. Nothing treads, and no one walks or moves. All is safe.

"Come along," he says. "Hurry," and they scurry.

"This way, Littlemouse, this way, Tinymouse," says Mothermouse. "Watch at your backs."

They eat both seed and leaf, crust and crumb, stem and stalk. They watch for footfall, feel for wingfall, test for trap, beware the pounce, the swoop, the snap.

Crack and crick go teeth, wavering goes whisker. Dangers in the dark must be heard and smelt, guessed and felt. Right is right, but wrong is…dead.

Youngmouse sees the stars. He sees the moon on a branch. He sees Flittermouse walk on the air with wings and hears him sing a shrill song.

I can only squeak, says Youngmouse to himself. And have only a tail. I wish I could be like Flittermouse. I wish I could. I'll go up and see.

He climbs to the woodshed roof. Flittermouse is higher still.

He climbs up on a trellis through the rambling rose. He pauses by a window. Cat is there behind the glass. She looks at him and gapes her mouth.

He sits above the window. Flittermouse floats by with black wing and black bright eye, a claw at every corner. Youngmouse looks up at him, and down.

The gutter is his next step, and then the roof. His claws are on the warm, dry tiles. All round he sees the city roofs, the streets with iron trees and fruits of light, the shiny twigs of rivers, the holes and homes where people live, the long animals on railway tracks.

Owl cries out, secret in the dark. On another rooftop yawns a cat, tuning for a song.

Flittermouse still flies above. "Look round," he says. "Look up, look down."

Youngmouse looks round, and nothing stirs but Flittermouse himself, running his dinner down and letting fall the mothy wings.

Youngmouse looks down. He feels his tail cling on.

"Look by, look by," calls Flittermouse, and turns away.

Youngmouse looks by, and by again. Above the garden is a shadow, wing and beak. Owl has come to hunt.

Far below, and calling to Youngmouse
are Littlemouse and Tinymouse, climbing
where he has climbed, on woodshed roof
and trellis. In the garden their Mothermouse
frantic, and Fathermouse wild, call for all three.

Youngmouse feels his back grow cold.
I have done wrong, he thinks. And wrong
is dead indeed, but not for me. For them.
What can I do?

Owl crosses the garden once. His
moonlight eyes swing from side to side.

Owl crosses the garden twice. His wings
gather silence.

Owl crosses the garden the third time,
and the last. He sees both Littlemouse and
Tinymouse playing in the moonlight.
Owl takes a quarter turn, rising a little,
getting ready.

On the roof Youngmouse cannot move,
because fear has made him solid. He cannot
call out. Dread has made him breathless.

Owl takes another quarter turn. His targets
are certain now; he cannot make an error.

Youngmouse gives a shriek. He jumps
from the roof, as if he had wings; as if, like
Flittermouse, he can fly.

The air holds him. If I had
wings, he thinks, I'd spread them
now, like this; and he holds out his limbs.
  Owl is dropping faster now, still silent.
Littlemouse and Tinymouse have seen him
in their sky, and with eyes tight shut they
crouch and wait, knowing they will die.
  Youngmouse spins down the air, as if
he walked. He bares his teeth and like
Flittermouse is fierce. He runs on air.
He sprints. He marathons.
  Owl puts out his talons, one for each
small mouse. Youngmouse does not stop
to think. He flies against Owl's face,
against his beak.
  Owl hoots out loud. He somersaults.
His flight has failed. Youngmouse topples
from the air upon the woodshed roof.

"Run quick away," he shouts. "Go home."
His sister and brother scamper to the edge
and down the wall.

Owl flies up again. He sees he lost two
little ones, but a middle-size one is left.
He swoops, and takes up speed. Over
Youngmouse he fills the sky, he fills the air.

Youngmouse waits and waits, until
Littlemouse and Tinymouse are safe below
with Fathermouse and Mothermouse.

He sees himself in Owl's grim eye,
coming down like fire. He waits until all
are safe below, and then he goes for home.

He leaps down the wall, as if he had wings again, and tumbles through the roses and among the kindling. Then he runs across the grass towards the cellar door.

Owl's last swoop touches his back with one sharp stroke, and Owl turns away from the house wall. With his cold shadow he turns to watch another garden. He shuts up his hunger-pointed claw.

"I flew, Papa," says Youngmouse, home at last with pain across his back.

"Nonsense," says Papa, "you're no Flittermouse, and are not to be."

"I flew, Mama," says Youngmouse. "I felt wings grow."

"Don't say such things," says Mothermouse. And where the Owl has touched she rubs a soothing ointment. "No more wings," she says. "Flittermouse is too flighty."

"Ah," says Youngmouse, in the nest content. He'll always know he flew; he always knew he could. Not high, not far, but well.

Outside Owl hunts on, Cat prowls, and Flittermouse sails to the moon.